MR. MEN
Adventure with
MONSTERS

Roger Hargreaves

Original concept by
Roger Hargreaves

Written and illustrated by
Adam Hargreaves

It was a dark and stormy night and Little Miss Scary and her friends were driving to the fair.

Little Miss Scary loved the fair. She loved all the scary rides and, best of all, she loved the ghost train.

Mr Jelly was not so excited.

However, as they were driving over the heath her scare-mobile suddenly spluttered and juddered to a halt.

"We've run out of petrol!" cried Mr Jelly.

"Whoops," said Mr Forgetful. "I knew there was something I meant to do."

The scare-mobile had broken down by a tall set of iron gates, opening onto a long driveway, leading up to a tall house, set on the hill.

"Shall we see if they can help?" suggested Little Miss Scary.

They all trudged up to the house in the wind and rain and knocked at the enormous front door.

With a loud groan, the door creaked open and silhouetted in the doorway stood a tall, bulky, square-headed figure.

"**Welcome. Do come in**," said the figure in a deep, rumbling voice.

Inside, in the light of the hallway, they saw their host more clearly.

He closed the door behind them with a loud bang.

Mr Jelly shook with fear. "It ... it's ... it's Frankenstein's Monster!" he stuttered.

They all shrieked and fled through the nearest doorway.

Little Miss Scary and her friends found themselves in a library, full of dusty bookshelves.

As they looked around, they heard a low moan and a ghost floated into the room through the wall!

Little Miss Giggles giggled nervously.

"Don't worry," said Mr Tickle. "It's only Little Miss Scary playing a trick. I know just how to sort this out."

He reached out his extraordinarily long arms to tickle the ghost, but his tickling fingers passed harmlessly right through it.

" **WOOAH!** " wailed the ghost.

"Help!" they all cried and ran from the room in different directions.

Little Miss Neat and Little Miss Quick rushed up the staircase into a bedroom.

A werewolf sat up in bed and a skeleton stepped out of the wardrobe.

"Yikes!" cried Little Miss Neat.

Quick as a flash, Little Miss Quick grabbed the skeleton's leg and tossed it out of the open window.

"Fetch!" she cried, and the werewolf leapt out of the window after the bone and the skeleton collapsed in a heap.

"That was quick thinking," said Little Miss Neat.

Meanwhile, Little Miss Scary and Mr Bump had fled into the bathroom.

But they were no safer.

There was a mummy soaking in the bath.

Mr Bump turned to escape from the room, but he slipped on the wet floor and landed with a great splash in the bath.

What a chaotic bundle of bandages!

At the very top of the house, Mr Greedy and Mr Jelly found themselves in a very dusty attic.

"I … I … I don't think this is any ordinary house," stammered Mr Jelly. "This is a haunted house!"

"What's that?" asked Mr Greedy, pointing at a shape hanging from the rafter. "Is it a bat?"

"That's not a bat!" shrieked Mr Jelly. "That's Dracula!"

"Welcome," said Dracula, with a very pointy-toothed grin.

Mr Jelly screamed and ran from the room, but Mr Greedy was not scared at all. And do you know why?

Mr Greedy had eaten three loaves of garlic bread for lunch. Everyone knows how much vampires hate garlic. And that's a lot of garlic!

It was Dracula's turn to be scared.

Everyone gathered out on the landing.

"We need to get out of here, fast!" trembled Little Miss Scary. And they all agreed.

Just then, the heavy clomp of Frankenstein's Monster's boots sounded on the stairs. He was not a very fast mover ...

Unlike Little Miss Quick.

"Quick! This way!" she cried, and led them down the back stairs into the kitchen ...

Where a slippery slobbery slime monster grinned at them from the sink!

And then with a loud slurp it hurled itself at them.

Everyone ran, but Mr Messy was not quick enough.

Mr Messy was now super slimy messy.

And green!

Poor Mr Jelly had not been able to keep up and he had got separated from the others.

He was all alone.

All alone in the haunted house!

As quiet as a mouse, he crept through the house until he found the cupboard under the stairs.

Inside the door there stood a huge pair of boots.

He climbed inside one of the huge boots and breathed a sigh of relief.

But Mr Jelly had not chosen a good hiding place …

Suddenly the boot he was in was lifted
and turned upside down and given a good shake.
Out fell Mr Jelly onto the floor.
It was the owner of the huge boots.
Big Foot!

"**Eeeek!**" screamed Big Foot, jumping up on a stool.

"It's a spider! No! It's a mouse! No! It's a … what are you?"

"I'm Mr Jelly," said Mr Jelly, who suddenly felt rather brave.

He had found someone even more frightened than he was!

All of Mr Jelly's friends had rushed into the living room.
It was a warm and cosy living room.

But they all shivered when they saw the large hairy figure
sitting on the sofa beside the fire.

It was the Abominable Snowman!

"**Welcome**," he growled.

The friends turned to escape, but Big Foot came stomping through the door towards them.

"Oh help! He's captured Mr Jelly!" yelled Little Miss Scary.

There was no escape! Little Miss Scary and her friends cowered in the corner.

And then in walked the skeleton, the ghost, the mummy and the werewolf. And finally, Frankenstein's monster …

… pushing a tea trolley!

"Anyone for tea?" he boomed.

"The monsters aren't scary at all" explained Mr Jelly. "They just wanted to invite us for tea!"

Mr Jelly grinned. It was not often that he was the least frightened person in a room.

"I'll be mother," said the mummy, and poured a cup of tea for everyone.

"One lump or two?" asked Dracula. "I have a very sweet tooth."

And they all had a jolly time toasting crumpets in front of the fire.

After tea, Frankenstein's Monster filled the scare-mobile with petrol, and they sped off to the fair, arriving before it closed.

Little Miss Scary looked at the scary roller coaster.

And she looked at the scary Ferris wheel.

And she looked at the scary helter skelter.

And then she looked at the very scary ghost train.

"Maybe it's time to go home," she said.

"I think we've had quite enough scares for one night!
Even for me!"

And everyone wholeheartedly agreed.